TROPICAL HAT TRICK

PIPER RAYNE

Tropical HAT TRICK

<u>**Hockey Hotties**</u>

Aiden Drake (Center)
My Lucky 13

Maksim Petrov (Defenseman)
The Trouble with #9

Ford Jacobs (Right Wing)
Faking it with #41

Warner Langley (Left Wing)
Sneaking around with #34

Cory Freeman (Center)
Second Shot with #76

Kane Burrows (Goalie)
Offside with #55

CHAPTER 1

Warner

"This is going to be sooo much fun!!" Nala clings to my arm the minute we arrive at the resort.

I stare down my former teammate, Casen. Nala is the best friend of Grey, Casen's girlfriend. The four of us are on vacation in the Caribbean since it's off-season.

Do I need this vacation?

Hell yes.

Should I have agreed to come here on some weird version of an extended double date?

Hell no.

But I'm here and I know exactly how Casen convinced me.

After I got traded last year to the Florida Fury, where my former best friend and now enemy plays, my job has been a source of constant stress and I could use some relaxation. Ford, my former best friend, only has *former* in the title because I fell in love with his sister. There's more to the story, but none of that matters right now.

The minute I saw Imogen at Ford's, it was as if my former life never existed. For years I pushed her out of my head, telling myself she's better off without me, but now that I'm playing with her brother again, all those feelings I pushed down for so long have erupted out of me.

And rumor is Imogen's moving to Florida to be closer to his daughter. Which means we're going to live in the same vicinity once again.

Everyone has that person—the one who tattoos themselves onto you. That's Imogen for me.

So I agreed to this ridiculous vacation as a way to get her off my mind. I'm not using Nala for sex though. I thought Casen knew me better than to bring a woman who's clearly a puck bunny with us. All she talks about is how hot she is, snapping photos of us and posting them on social media. Which Casen knows I fucking hate.

"Did I tell you I was named after *The Lion King*?"

"I thought the lion king was named Simba?" Casen says, handing his credit card to the woman behind the resort's check-in desk.

"That's the male lion. I was his best friend, Nala. My dad always said he named me that because I was fit to be a princess."

"I think I'm missing something," Casen says.

I'm more than happy to let him take the reins on this.

Thankfully, one of the other hotel employees hangs up the phone and waves me over to his computer.

"Langley. Just checking in."

He types on the keyboard.

"She wasn't a princess," Casen corrects Nala.

"He's the king after his dad dies, but I couldn't be the queen because his mom was alive still."

"Wait!" Grey holds up her hand and I wonder if maybe the teacher in her still thinks summer break hasn't started. "Are we assuming Nala and Simba married?"

"I have your room, Mr. Langley."

Luckily, the employee gives me an out of this stupid conversation about a Disney movie. The only thing I'm getting from it is that Nala wants to be a queen, which only cements my theory of her being a puck bunny.

"Do you have a room right next to his?" Nala knocks me in the shoulder when she comes beside me.

I step aside and give the man a look that says if he does, he's a dead man. I take my key card before she can see what room I'm in. I'm going to walk her to her room, then I'll go to mine so she never figures it out.

"Let me check. What's your full name?" After she gives it to him, his fingers type along the keyboard. "I'm very sorry, ma'am, but you've booked a garden view room and Mr. Langley's is oceanfront. Would you like to upgrade your stay?"

Thank fuck.

"Oh." Nala's smile dims. "Um, no. Thank you though."

Guilt eats at my stomach lining. I hate seeing someone feel lesser than because they can't afford what's deemed the best.

With a sigh, I ask, "Do you have any oceanfront rooms?"

The man's perfectly sculpted eyebrows crinkle. "Let me check."

"Hey, we're all checked in. See you in twenty down by the pool." Casen and Grey get on a golf cart and drive away with their guide to their room.

I give them a wave.

"We do have one. Right next to you actually, Mr. Langley." He smiles.

I try to do the same, but it probably looks more like a cringe. I take out my credit card and slide it over the counter. "Go ahead and charge my card."

"Oh, thank you!" Nala lifts on her tiptoes and kisses my cheek. "My own knight in shining armor."

I huff and the man behind the desk smiles to himself.

"You're very lucky, Nala, because I wasn't sure I'd be able to move you. We have a high-profile wedding here this week and most of our rooms are booked up."

"Oh, a wedding." Nala rests her cheek on my shoulder. "What a beautiful place to get married. Would you do a destination wedding?"

"I don't plan on getting married." I slide her her room card and pick up my bag, heading over to the golf cart.

The bellhop takes our bags.

She slides in next to me on the golf cart. "What do you mean you don't want to get married, silly?" She playfully swats me.

Imogen used to do that. She'd pinch me in the bicep when I joked with her.

"Exactly that. I don't want to get married."

Her lips turn down, but then she smiles. "You just have to meet the right girl." She pokes me in the side with her finger.

"No, that's not it."

"Yes, it is." She pokes me again.

"No, it's not."

"A guy like you has to reproduce. You can't leave your gorgeous and talented gene pool not replicated."

God, this woman doesn't stop. Annoyance grates on my last nerve of the day.

"That's the great thing about it being my life, Nala, I can do whatever the hell I want." The bellhop stops the golf cart, and I get out and grab my bag, then tip the man. "I've got my bag, please just take care of her."

With that, I head upstairs to my room, eager to be free of her.

"Don't forget the pool, Warner!" she calls.

I raise my hand back at her without turning around. "Got it."

I'm busy shaking my head in annoyance as I walk up the steps and run right into a big body.

"Shit. Sorry," I mumble. I look up and—you have to be kidding me. "Drake?"

I have to blink. Aiden Drake is standing in front of me in board shorts and flip-flops. Since he's Ford's new best friend, I have an inkling whose wedding the hotel employee was talking about—Ford's.

That's one hell of a coincidence and if I were another man, I might think of it as fate.

"Crashing the wedding?" Aiden asks with a smirk.

Ford might just put me in the hospital when he finds out I'm here, but even so, all I can think about is the fact that Imogen is here somewhere and she's probably wearing a bikini.

CHAPTER 2

"Hey, ladies."

Jana

"**W**hy must they play volleyball all day?" I'm on the ledge of the pool, the sun heating my shoulders, and stare at all the men we're on vacation with hijacking the beach volleyball area once again.

Paisley, my best friend and Maksim's girlfriend, laughs. "You're telling me you're not appreciative of all those bare chests?"

"Shouldn't you only be looking at one bare chest?" I ask and raise an eyebrow.

She laughs again. "I only care about one bare chest, but I can appreciate the fact that we're in a tropical paradise with a bunch of hockey hotties." She sips her frozen cocktail.

"We've grown up with hockey hotties, remember?"

My dad owns the professional hockey team, the Florida Fury, and since I've known Paisley since forever, we grew up admiring the build of a hockey player. Which is probably why she fell for Maksim. But Maksim is one of the good ones. He looks at my best friend as though all his happiness is in her hands. It's endearing, but like I said, he's rare.

Actually, most of the hockey men here are a rare species. Maksim and Paisley are one of three couples who've fallen madly in love over the past year. It's like there's something in the water in the team locker room.

First Aiden Drake, then Maksim, and now we're here to witness the nuptials between Ford and Lena. Which is funny since Ford was a known womanizer before his relationship with Lena. The guy couldn't keep his pants zipped or his fists from fighting off the ice. Lena must have a magic va-jay-jay to keep Ford in line.

"Aren't you the one who told me that there are good hockey players out there?" Paisley asks before taking another sip of her frozen drink.

"Because I wanted you to put yourself out there and look, it worked." I lift her hand where her engagement ring rests. Her very large, very sparkly engagement ring.

She smiles and holds it up, allowing the sun to cast rays on it. "Exactly. So I only feel as though it's right for me to do the same for you."

I swim back over to the bar, ignoring her.

"Hey, don't swim off." She follows, holding her drink above the water.

"Can I have another daiquiri?" I ask the bartender.

The young guy behind the bar smiles, checks out my cleavage in my bikini, and fills my order, giving me extra cherries. Something tells me that if he plays his cards right, he might just find himself in bed with me one of these nights.

"Stop dodging the obvious. I know you like Kane Burrows."

I glance around. "Stop it. My dad owns the team."

We head back toward the ledge we were using. The one that gives us the best view of the volleyball courts. Aiden Drake just made his appearance with the boys.

"Where are all the girls anyway?" I look over at the pool loungers.

"Saige went to help Lena to figure out the rehearsal dinner," Paisley says.

"Shouldn't Ford have gone?" I ask with what I'll admit is judgment.

"Lena was happy to do it on her own and give Ford time with his friends."

"Uh-huh." I sip my drink.

"Back to Kane Burrows." Once again, she sounds as though she's practically yelling his name.

"Will you please lower your voice? Besides, that was, like, ten years ago, when he was young and in shape."

We look at the volleyball court where Kane, a.k.a. Zeus to the hockey world, is spiking a ball over the net.

Paisley eyes him. "That man is not out of shape."

She has a point, but I'll deny it. When my dad told me he traded Kane to the Fury last year, I spit out my martini in the middle of a party. Literally. Yes, I had a massive crush on Kane when he first joined the league back in the day. I think it was the fact that he's from Canada and therefore, in my mind, very polite and considerate. Not to mention that he epitomizes the strong, silent type. He's physically big and generally pretty quiet, but he has a huge presence when he walks into a room.

"He has a gut," I say, staring into my daiquiri.

Paisley laughs. "What gut? Seriously, you're making shit up."

"Think about this, Paisley. He's a professional hockey player at the tail end of his career. He's maybe got one more year in him, max. And yet no family, no children, no attachments. He's not one of the good ones."

She pretends to think it over. "Maybe he just hasn't met the right person."

"In how many years? Fifteen?" The skepticism in my tone can't be missed.

She shrugs a tanned shoulder. "Maybe he's just waiting on you."

And then, out of nowhere, Kane Burrows turns in our direction. He says something to the guys, then walks toward us.

"And here he comes, the hockey player voted best looking on the blog *Hockey Hotties*." Paisley pretends to be an announcer, speaking loudly into her fist.

I groan. "Please stop."

"Hey, ladies," Kane says when he approaches the bar at the side of the pool. "Enjoying the water?" He looks down with this grin as if to say he wants to join us.

"Hey, Kane. Another volleyball game? Haven't you boys had enough of that?" Paisley asks.

"Are you kidding? We're on an island and none of us are the sunbathing, drink pina colada type of guys. You do know your soon-to-be husband, right?" He laughs and signs the slip for a bucket of beers.

"Maksim can't sit still long enough to watch my favorite rom-com."

I stare at Kane, appreciating his rugged appeal. Most hockey players are what you'd consider manly, but Kane even more so. Between his close-trimmed beard, his chin-length chestnut hair, and his muscles, he looks part lumber-jack, part *GQ* model.

"Try an action flick next time and I bet he sits through it." He picks up the bucket of beers. "Why don't you ladies come play with us?"

"Nah, we'll leave that for you guys." Paisley waves him off.

"Kotik!" Maksim yells from the court.

Kane squats. "Looks like you're wanted. Don't worry, I'm happy to take care of Jana."

My stomach shouldn't ignite with flutters over the fact that he knows my name. I'm his boss's daughter and I work in the organization. Of course he knows my name.

"I don't need anyone to take care of me," I say with attitude to mask my attraction to him.

He stares at me for a moment. "Okay then. You know where to find me when you change your mind." He winks, stands, and walks away, looking over his shoulder one more time before he reaches the guys.

"I'm going to play. Come on." Paisley climbs out of the water, picking up her drink.

"I'll watch, but I'm not playing."

I climb out after her and we saunter over to the men. Maksim wraps Paisley in a hug, and I sit on the ledge of the brick wall, letting my feet dangle.

"You sure?" Kane asks, spinning the ball on his finger.

"Yeah."

He serves the ball to the other side, and yeah, there's only one solution to get him out of my system... and that's to sleep with him.

CHAPTER 3

*"I need to hire a hype woman and
you're going to be her."*

Imogen

Afterwe get the rehearsal dinner all set, Saige, Lena, and I change into our swimsuits and head down to the beach and pool area. My parents are here and watching my niece, Annabelle, for Ford and Lena, so I decide to head to the pool bar to grab a drink for something to do.

This is our second day here and although I love the States, I wouldn't mind disappearing from my life and living down here. I order the bartender's special daiquiri and notice him check out my cleavage when he hands it over.

Maybe I should just flirt back and have fun while I'm here. If only my mind wasn't preoccupied with two things. One, that I have no job lined up after I relocate to Florida to be closer to Ford, Lena, and Annabelle. Two, that I ended up in a serious make-out session that almost led to sex at my niece's birthday party.

The kiss was a giant mistake that my entire family found out about when Warner and I came down the stairs at the same time and found everyone staring at us, rather than outside around the pool.

Warner had asked to talk to me, and I'd just wanted to get the awkwardness of us being in the same world again over with. But damn it all to hell, I'd had a few drinks and my hormones went crazy from one apology and one flirtatious grin of his.

Ugh. I push that out of my head and sip my daiquiri on the way over to the beach volleyball court where all the Florida Fury players have been spending their time since we arrived.

Jana, who happens to be the owner of the team's daughter, is sitting on the ledge of the brick wall, watching them. Now there's a woman who has it all together. She doesn't take shit from anyone. When I grow up, I want to be her.

"Hey, Imogen," she says and pats the spot next to her.

"Hey, Jana." I raise up the same daiquiri that she's holding. "They're good."

She chuckles. "Yeah, they are, and the bartender is good for the self-esteem."

My head falls back in laughter. I guess I'm not the only one he flirts with. I wonder how many women he gets into his bed while working here. Nothing wrong with a vacation fling.

"Very true." I sip my daiquiri and slide up onto the ledge. "Who's winning?"

"Kane's team," she says with a growl.

"Do we not like Kane?" I ask, turning my head away from the game to see her reaction.

She shrugs. "We're indifferent. But I do have to figure out a way to market a player who's probably in his last year in the league."

"I don't think there's anything hard about marketing Kane Burrows. He's like the godfather of hockey. Sure, he's aging, but your dad wouldn't have drafted him if he didn't still have it. He set the record for most blocks last year. Not to mention the wisdom he can impart on the team from his experience."

She says nothing and my face heats—and not from the tropical sun trying to break through my sunblock. I should've kept my thoughts to myself. What do I know about marketing a hockey team anyway?

Jana leans back on her hands, and her gaze falls to the giant of a man. I remember when he played for New York. Ford and Warner were all about him, wanting to go to every game. Kane really is a legend in the sport.

"Tell me one thing you'd do to drive people to the games," Jana says, her voice all business now.

My heart rate picks up from being put on the spot. "Oh, I'm not a marketing person or anything."

"You clearly love hockey and know a lot about it." She looks at me from the corner of her eyes, still not stripping her gaze off of Kane.

"Well, Ford's played since forever and I ended up following it too. We'd fight over the remote until I started enjoying the games. The fights are what got me at first, to be honest."

She laughs. "That gets most people. Plus, a hockey guy is always in shape."

"It's weird, right? Even though they're covered in pads, it's still better than football and those tight pants."

She laughs. "So true. You should come in sometime and watch them when they arrive in their suits. Let me tell you, that Warner Langley knows how to wear one of those. And since his one sponsor is Hildenburg Watches, he's always got the bling on. There's something sexy about that."

I remain silent because I've seen the pictures, so I know exactly what she means. Hello, I have Google and on occasion, my willpower wanes. He's definitely not the shy boy I spent late nights in my parents' theater room with anymore. I have a feeling he knows how to use that mouth and those hands to satisfy a woman to complete exhaustion. Although I enjoyed the shy boy with tentative hands too.

"Huh. I've never noticed him." I'm not sure why I'm lying to Jana, but the sideways glance she gives me tells me she must know something.

"Sorry to break it to you, but I was at Ford's birthday party for Annabelle."

I sigh. "I know."

"I saw the way Warner had eyes on you the entire day. Plus, I might have been in the kitchen when the two of you went upstairs." She faces me fully and I quickly twist my head to stare at the volleyball court.

Train is now arguing with Ford about a ball hitting the line and Kane is playing referee.

She knocks her shoulder against mine. "If you want to talk about it, I'm here. God knows, I have a few more years of experience."

I tuck my hands under my thighs and rock. An old habit that reappears whenever someone asks me about Warner and what went down. "There isn't much to tell. He and Ford played together back in the day."

"And the reason they hate one another?"

I can't give the dirt to the owner's daughter. Ford would kill me. "You know guys, their egos get in the way sometimes."

"Well, it'll be interesting watching them play on the same team. Last year, Warner wasn't on the same line as Ford except for a few times. This year, my dad..." She looks toward the volleyball court and lowers her tone. "Warner's being moved up to Ford's line. Tweetie is moving down."

My gut twists because surely the fights on the ice are now going to involve teammates rather than competitors. I'm not even sure I can stand to watch any of the games now.

Ford can't let the past go. You'd think he was the one left behind.

"Anyway, let's get back to Kane Burrows," Jana says. "Actually, all three of the new players need to be marketed to our fans. Especially since Drake, Petrov, and your brother have all settled down. We need the single guys to step up." She sips her daiquiri, and one thing is for sure, she's always got her eye on Kane. Currently, he's wiping sand off his magnificent abs that do not look like they belong to the oldest player in hockey.

"It's easy—you take a picture of that." I motion to Kane.

We both laugh.

"In all seriousness, you play to the hype of the player," I say, getting into the idea. "Kane Burrows is known for being a goalie you can't get past. Market him by the stats, make him into the legend he already is. People love a legend, and they especially want to see them do great things when they're at the end of their career."

She nods. "And Cory?"

"Easy. He's young, fast, and hungry. Hungry to make a name for himself. Play on the fact that he's the up-and-comer they want to root for."

"I won't ask about Warner Langley since he's a sensitive topic around the Jacobs family. But can I ask you what your plans are now that you're living in Florida?"

I shrug. "I'll need to find something to occupy my time. I'll probably end up being Annabelle's nanny until I figure out something more long term."

She sips her daiquiri and shakes her head. "No, you won't, because you're coming to work for the Florida Fury. I need to hire a hype woman and you're going to be her."

I choke on my own daiquiri and shake my head. "What?"

"I promise the pay is great, and you'll get to spend lots of time with the hockey players. You obviously know how to sell people and I don't want to hire someone who doesn't know anything about the sport. The players won't respect them."

"Are you serious?" I hate the fact that I love it. The job sounds perfect for me.

"Yeah, but there's one thing you need to realize before accepting the job."

"What?"

She nods farther down the beach. "Can you work alongside him? Because we will be heavily marketing that guy."

I follow her vision and my jaw drops open. "Is that Warner?"

"What?" Ford whips around as if he has superpower hearing when it comes to his mortal enemy's name. He looks at the spot on the beach where Warner is.

I hop off the ledge to try to head this off.

"One day you're going to give me the skinny on this situation!" Jana yells after me while I try to reach Ford before he does something he shouldn't.

Lucky for me, half of the team is right there with me.

Still, what is Warner doing here? And why does he have to be in board shorts and looking as mouthwatering as always?

Chapter 4

"Hockey players and their egos."

Kane

The egos on these young players never cease to amaze me. I thought it was childish that Ford didn't invite Warner in the first place when the rest of the team was invited. But Warner showing up here uninvited? What is this, middle school? I know there's a beef there and I'm pretty sure it goes way back and involves Ford's sister, Imogen. If that's the case, I give Ford a pass on his childish behavior because family loyalty comes first.

I jog over on the hot sand since Ford looks ready to tackle Warner to the ground. In the age of social media, we do not need someone taking pictures of two Florida Fury players wrestling in the sand or drowning each other in the ocean.

I'm annoyed by this pending altercation because I love the way Jana was checking me out. She's trying to act as though she doesn't like me, but we both know she's lying to herself. The minute her old man traded for me, and I sat across the table from her, that undeniable pull was there. Although she's ignoring it.

"What the hell are you doing here?" Ford hollers once he reaches Warner.

Warner holds up his hands and eyes Aiden Drake, who's next to Ford.

Ford looks at Drake. "You had something to do with this?"

Drake backs up. "Hell no. I just ran into him."

"And you didn't tell me?"

"We were having such a great day. I figured it's a big resort, maybe you wouldn't see one another."

Everyone laughs, including Drake. I'm sure he didn't want to be the one to deliver the bad news—shoot the messenger and all that.

I move myself closer, ready to stop the fight if one begins. Mr. Gerhardt told me that he wants me to have a role in the locker room since I have so much experience. He wants me to be the one who offers guidance to my team-mates, especially the younger players. I'm not an idiot and I know my time as a player is coming to an end; taking on that role might help me decide whether I'd ever want to coach one day.

"Listen. I didn't..." Warner stops talking when Imogen joins the group and stands next to Ford. "Know this is where you were getting married. I'm here with Casen and his girl-friend and her..."

Imogen's shoulders fall before rising back up, masking her initial reaction.

"Warner!" a woman screeches from down the beach.

"Holy shit," Maksim murmurs.

We all watch as a woman in a swimsuit that hardly has enough material to be considered a bikini jogs down the beach as if she's on *Baywatch*. Which I won't bother mentioning because I'm likely the only one here who remembers that show.

Warner looks over his shoulder and cringes. "She's Casen's girlfriend's friend." Then he eyes Imogen. "We're staying in separate rooms."

Ford steps in front of his sister, clearly taking a protective stance. "She doesn't care."

"What's going on?" Lena weaves through the group. "Warner…" She sighs.

Meanwhile, the *Baywatch* girl arrives and hooks her arm through Warner's, staring wide eyed at the rest of us. "Kane Burrows? Aiden Drake? Oh my god, I'm a huge fan."

Warner rolls his eyes. "This is Nala."

"I don't give a shit." Ford crosses his arms.

Lena puts her hand on her soon-to-be-husband's fore-arm. "Just relax." Lena was the Jacobs' family PR rep, so she steps between us and them. "This isn't the best coincidence, but this is also a big resort. So, you keep your distance, and we'll keep ours. Have a great vacation, Warner and Nala." She smiles brightly.

Ford growls behind her and Imogen slides out from behind her brother. Her eyes fall to Nala, coasting down the woman's body since it's on display for all to see.

"Congratulations," Warner says to Lena. "Let's go."

I notice that Warner doesn't take Nala's hand while the two of them walk down the beach.

"I can't fucking believe this," Ford mumbles, walking back to the volleyball court. Everyone follows him, except for Imogen, who watches Warner for a minute more. Warner looks over his shoulder once before heading up the beach to the other pool area.

I can't imagine what this season is going to bring. Drama probably. Lots of it.

I head back to the volleyball court and Jana waves me over to her. Just when I thought I'd have to keep flirting with her until the wedding and then finally make my big move, she makes her move.

"Hey," I say, leaning along the brick ledge she's been

hanging out on. Her skin is golden brown already and glistening from the sweat or sun protection she's wearing. It only makes her look like the goddess she expects to be treated as.

"All handled?"

I shake my head. "Hell no. Pretty sure that was just the beginning. Warner, at the same resort as Ford, is like putting two cocks together."

"Excuse me?"

"You know, roosters."

"Oh."

"Dirty mind?" I ask, clearly joking, but she straightens her back.

"We just don't need the bad press, you know?"

I move away from the wall, unsure how to handle her. "I didn't realize I'm the Fury PR person. Maybe you should've been down there to handle it."

"You put yourself in the middle. I saw it from here."

"Because I wasn't going to let Ford have a black eye in his wedding pictures."

She brings her daiquiri to her plump lips and covers the straw, dramatically sucking the frozen drink. She's playing games with me. "How very noble of you."

"What's your game here?" I ask.

I've always preferred a straightforward woman. I don't mind the chase, but once I catch her, I consider us to be at the finish line, not passing the baton off for the next section of the race.

I learned my lesson young that when you're a professional athlete, women don't always love you for you, they love you for what you can give them. Whether that's money, security, or just the bit of fame that comes from being with you.

"Game? I don't play games," Jana says.

"That's funny, I thought for sure you were checking me out earlier."

"You're mistaken." She looks at the ocean as if I'm boring her.

Everything inside me says this will not end well, but here I am. Maybe I didn't learn my lesson. Though I know I don't have anything Jana would want as far as money or fame. She has it in spades because of who her dad is.

"How about this? If I win this volleyball game, you sit with me at dinner tonight."

She flips her hair over her shoulder. "And why would I do that?"

"Because you want to."

"You're pretty cocky for a guy who's almost about to hang up his skates."

I tilt my head and move closer to her. Lowering my voice, I say, "And you're pretty arrogant for a woman who's dying for me to make her come, but just won't admit it."

Her eyes widen for a beat, then she gives me a mocking laugh. "Hockey players and their egos."

"It's our egos that help us fuck the way we do. Remember that when you're lying in bed alone tonight."

Before she can say anything, I push off the brick wall and head back to the game. She'll come around.

CHAPTER 5

"Don't pretend there aren't mirrors in your house."

Ande

 wall of humidity hits us when we step out of the airport, even though it's nine at night.

"Jesus, it's hot." Sophie waves her hand at her already red face. "I feel queasy." She hooks her arm through mine, then stumbles. I right her before she falls flat on her face.

The person who should be half in the bag, stuttering and on the verge of throwing up, is me. The shots on the plane should've been mine. But my best friend took it upon herself to start my girls' "better off without him" party all by herself.

"Soph, you're such a lightweight," Brit says, her accusatory finger pointed. "We need to catch that bus to our resort, otherwise we'll be stuck here all night. One time when I came down with my brother..."

She continues to recount her story while walking in front of us like our designated tour guide. Sophie and I exchange a look to say Brit's already starting. Hell, she started as soon as we reached the airport in Tampa. She was even lecturing a half-asleep Sophie about what's going to happen when we arrive at the airport while we were sliding into our Uber.

We all have our roles in our threesome. Brit is the planner, the organizer. In college, she bought our groceries, paid our bills, and left little notes on the dry erase board to let us know what we owed.

Sophie is the neurotic one. Hence the drunk version of herself right now. Did you think I'd say she's the partier? Nope. She got drunk because she hates to fly. She obsesses over every little thing outside her control. Which makes Brit the perfect friend for her. She plans so much, Sophie never has to worry about what-ifs with her around.

As for me? Well, I used to be the "head in the clouds, daydreaming" kind of gal until my college boyfriend broke my heart six months ago. Now my mantra is that romance sucks and every man is only out to use you for as long as he needs/wants you. Not a healthy attitude by any means, but you should've heard me during my anger phase.

"Let's go, Candy Ande, we're not going to make it!" Brit yells.

"Well, I'm lugging about one hundred and twenty pounds!" I yell, earning glares from the other people waiting for buses to take them to their hotels in this mecca of transportation vehicles. "Come on, Soph, you gotta walk."

"I'm tired. I never should've taken my anxiety medicine and drank."

"You didn't... oh, Soph." I stare down at her since she's inches shorter than me unless she's wearing heels.

She nods as Brit runs back to us after handing her luggage to the bus driver. "Just give me your suitcase."

"You could take Sophie," I suggest, but Brit's already back at the attendant, handing over my luggage. "Or not."

"She's so bossy, but I love her so much." Sophie rests her cheek on my upper arm, staring up at me like a little girl.

"Who knows what we would do if she wasn't here."

It's the truth. I rely on Brit in situations like this. She

probably virtually mapped our path before we arrived—five times over.

"*Hola*, Raul," Sophie says, rolling her *r*'s because she was the president of the Spanish honor society in high school. She's supposed to be our interpreter on this trip.

"Hola," he says, and Sophie leans forward like she has a secret. Raul steps back.

"It's okay, I speak fluent Spanish." She spins and points to everyone around us. "We can hold a conversation."

Raul stares at her, then widens his eyes at Brit and me.

"But maybe now isn't the time for that." Brit tugs Sophie up the stairs and into a seat, then proceeds to sit next to her, giving her the bottle of water she bought at the gift shop and the plastic bag it came in.

"Finally, I'm off the babysitting shift." I scour the large bus, searching for a spot without a head popping up over the back of the seat in front of it, but the bus is packed full. I'd rather be near my friends, but I'll settle for any seat.

"You can sit here," a deep voice says from behind me.

Brit peeks around me and her eyes widen.

Great. I can't read whether her expression is good or bad.

"You're a cutie," Sophie says to him. Apparently her usual shyness was drowned in mini bottles of vodka on the plane.

I slowly turn and he stretches out his arm, removing a backpack from the empty seat beside him.

"Thank you." I slide in with only a quick glance his way because Sophie has already embarrassed us enough.

"No problem," he says, his deep voice eliciting a shiver up my spine.

I sit and put my oversized purse in my lap. He fumbles

with his phone between his legs, a text message screen up. Other than noticing his strong, tawny-colored hands and the tattoos covering his forearms, I don't catch much about him.

He sighs, and I instinctively glance over. His hands are kind of sexy. Hands don't usually get me going, but I do appreciate short, trimmed nails and those veins that bulge just slightly out of the skin on the forearms. I mentally note no wedding ring. Not that I should care. I'm in no shape to have a man in my life, no matter how briefly.

"Excuse me," he says.

My eyes slide up the corded muscles in his forearms to his bulging biceps and over his broad shoulders to a set of stunning brown eyes. He's all strong jaw, high cheekbones wrapped in beautiful warm-bronze skin.

"Do you know?"

Shit, I was gawking and now I have no idea what he asked me.

"Yep, you're on the right one. We're going there too," Brit interjects, her head peering over the back of our seats.

He nods. "Thanks."

I watch him hammer out a text to someone, then his phone vibrates every millisecond as his screen pings one text after another. He sighs again and turns off the screen, ignoring the vibrating.

Busy man, I guess.

The two of us sit in silence. Sophie's groaning and Brit's lecturing her is the only conversation on the bus filled with travel-weary passengers.

"Okay, guys, cool it," I whisper.

Sophie sighs and puts her head against the window, while Brit rolls her eyes. But at least they both quiet down.

"Have you been there before?" The deep timbre of the

voice next to me undoes something inside me that I can't explain.

"Where's that?" I ask.

He chuckles and I realize he's talking about the resort we're staying at.

"Oh, the resort?" I glance over and make eye contact. He truly is a beautiful man. He nods, a smile tipping the corner of his lips. I find myself waiting for his full lips to open completely, but they don't. "No. But my friend Brit can probably rattle off any fact you'd like to know. She's like having your own personal travel guide."

He turns slightly in his seat and glances back at Brit. Following his vision, I find her scouring through papers.

She looks up, probably sensing our eyes on her. "What?"

He laughs and falls back into the seat. "Always a good thing to have a friend like that."

I nod. He's not wrong. It's nice never having to plan things when we're together. Although sometimes her stress ups my anxiety. "Once we get there, I'll force-feed her a few drinks and she'll relax."

"I'd love to find a bed, but I'm pretty sure my friends will force-feed me some drinks too." As he says it, his phone vibrates again.

"Guys' trip?"

"No. I'm here for a wedding. But all my tea—friends are here too, and it might turn more into a guys' trip if someone doesn't keep them in line." There's a fleeting look, as though he's holding something back.

Not that I'm stellar at reading people. I couldn't even read that my jackass ex was coming home late from being out with another woman rather than working late.

I nod.

"Is it just you three girls?" he asks.

"Yeah."

"Well, I will apologize for my... friends. They can get rowdy and loud. Let's just say you'll probably hear us before you see us."

As though he knew exactly what his friends would do, the bus pulls up to our resort and a bunch of guys are outside with drinks in their hands, hooting and hollering "Free Man" at the bus.

His head falls forward and he shakes it. "See what I mean?"

Everyone on the bus stares.

Brit's head turns toward me. "Holy shit."

Brit won't say it, but Sophie would if she were awake. The guys standing outside the bus are all hot. Every single one has big muscles and a cocky arrogance that somehow makes them more appealing.

I raise my eyebrows at Brit, and she hits me in the elbow and whispers, "Rebound material, Candy Ande."

She grabs her bag and coaxes Sophie up and out of her seat because Brit wants to be the first one to check in. I see the competitiveness on her face.

Then the guy next to me stands, and my gaze travels from his chest up to his rich-brown eyes that hold a flirtatious glint mixed with embarrassment.

"Sorry about them," he mumbles.

"No need," I say. "Tell me though, do you and your friends play beach volleyball?"

Brit cracks up, bending over and laughing, jolting a comatose Sophie.

"I'm not sure I understand the joke?" he says, starting down the row toward the exit.

"Oh, you shouldn't."

"*Top Gun*, big guy," Brit says, walking down the stairs and dragging Sophie toward the check-in desk.

"Ah... so you want to see me shirtless and sweaty?" He stops right outside the bus to retrieve his luggage.

My face heats. "Don't act like you don't have mirrors in your house."

The bellhop from the resort pulls out our luggage. He hands the stranger a large duffel bag, and he puts it sideways over his body.

"Let me help with these," the handsome man says, taking Brit's and Sophie's large suitcases.

"You travel light," I say.

"Can't say the same about you."

"Touché, but it takes a lot for us women to look good."

His crazy group of friends grow louder as we approach. He leans in, leaving the luggage right outside the doors of the resort.

"Ah, don't pretend there aren't mirrors in *your* house." He winks and clicks his tongue against the roof of his mouth before his friends swallow him up.

"What the fuck, Jet? Why the hell would you take the bus to the resort?" one of the guys asks.

He ducks his head and looks back one more time before a girl surprises him by jumping into his arms. Then all of his friends, and the girl who could be his girlfriend, head toward the bar area.

CHAPTER 6

"I'm one lucky bastard."

Lena

A finger runs down my spine toward my ass.

Smack!

"Ford!" I don't move because his hands smooth over where he just smacked me. I groan and roll over. "What if I was actually asleep?"

He props up on his elbow and rests his head in his palm. "Two more days and you're a Jacobs." He leans forward and kisses my nose.

"I can't wait. Do you think we should've just eloped? I mean, this is starting to feel like a lot."

He rolls on top of me, using his knees to make room for himself.

God, I love this man.

"Well, think of it this way, we have thirty-plus babysitters for Annabelle, so I can wake up and do this." He bends down and kisses my neck. "And this." He travels down my body, kissing every inch of skin. "And this." He sucks my nipple into his mouth, and I suck in a breath.

I arch and moan, gliding my fingers up his muscular back. He continues to travel down my body until he puts both of my legs over his shoulders.

"If we didn't bring anyone, I wouldn't be able to do this." He swipes his tongue up along my folds and I bolt off the mattress, then fall back down, enjoying every touch this man gifts me with.

It's corny to say, but no one before him had the same talent. Which I know is probably because there were a lot of women in Ford's life before me—more than the men I ever had—but I'm the one who got the ring. I'm the one he looks at every morning with love. So I don't care where he learned it. This man loves me fully and wholeheartedly—with his heart and his tongue.

He sucks my nub, twirling his tongue around, and his hands venture up to my breasts and squeeze them. His thumbs run over my peaked nipples, and I moan from the stirring low in my abdomen. Ford is right. If we were at home, we would never get to enjoy this right now.

Our fourteen-month-old gets up at the crack of dawn. Most times, we'll just be getting started and hear her over the monitor. Ford tried to turn it off once, threw a toy in the crib, but she only grew louder because she is nothing if not her father's daughter.

I love our sex at night, but it doesn't compare to the morning.

Lowering one hand, he teases my opening with the tip of his finger, and I cry out for it.

"Please, Ford. Just come up here and fuck me."

He shakes his head between my legs, the shadow of a beard from his vacation causing a delicious friction along my thighs. He continues to torment me with one finger, then another, arching them to hit me just right.

"Oh, God," I say, and he chuckles.

My arrogant fiancé loves when I cry out because of what he calls "his skills."

I grip his hair and he doesn't change his tempo, knowing what I need more than I do. I need him to continue what he's doing for a little bit longer before changing it up. When I first got with Ford, I loved the way he made me feel when we had sex, but he's learned what works for me and what I need, and it's gotten even better over time. Talk about a sexy man.

I wiggle under him, and he holds one hand on my pelvis to keep me steady. I relish every second of his domineering nature. I pull on his hair and he increases the speed, while I grind and ride his tongue until my head falls back and stars burst behind my closed eyelids. I attempt to close my legs, but he makes sure to help me ride the wave back down until I'm lying there like a heap of flesh.

He wipes his mouth with the back of his hand before crawling up my body and hovering over me. "Now what were you saying about eloping?"

"Just fuck me, Ford."

"Gladly." He smirks, gliding into my wetness, thrusting as deep as he can get. "Damn, you feel so good."

I wrap my legs around his waist, my second orgasm already edging closer.

Ford doesn't relent because we both know how turned on he gets when he makes me come first. He does this rolling hip action and that orgasm that was close becomes imminent. I cling to his biceps, my nails digging into his skin.

He rises on his hands, not putting any weight on me, and watches himself gliding in and out of me. "You're so fucking sexy and you're going to be my wife. All mine."

"Yours," I pant, clenching to keep the orgasm from coming so soon.

"And I'm yours, babe." His thumb runs along my lips. "All yours."

That's it. I combust for a second time this morning and

Ford pumps into me a few more times and stills, falling on top of me. He brushes the hair off my forehead and kisses me gently as he continues to come inside me.

"I love you," he says sweetly.

I wrap my arms around his shoulders and hold him. "I love you."

Ford eventually gets up, and I go into the bathroom to clean myself up when there's a knock on the door.

"Go away!" Ford shouts.

I come out of the bathroom and give him the look.

"Daddy. I woke up Aiden and Saige at three in the morning." Aiden pretends to be Annabelle behind the door.

I hurry and put on a robe, while Ford throws on his shorts from last night, going to the door. He swings the door open and there stands an exhausted-looking Aiden with Annabelle draped over him. Ford grabs her. She's passed out, making the exchange easier.

"I'm sorry, and tell Saige we're sorry," I say to him with a grimace.

He waves me off. "Don't worry, I plan on knocking her up with quadruplets and making you babysit them when I wanna fuck her at our destination wedding." He hands me the diaper bag. "See you guys later. Oh, Saige says she'll be ready in an hour to go talk to that person about the rehearsal. I'll be asleep."

Aiden walks away while I repeatedly apologize before shutting the door.

Ford's in one of the hotel chairs, Annabelle lying on his naked chest like a koala bear. I take a moment to soak in the picture. It wasn't that long ago that I never would've envisioned living this life that I love so much.

Never did I think I would be with Ford, much less raise

his daughter as my own alongside him. I really did hit the jackpot.

"She's out cold. She just needs to nap with Daddy." He leans his head back and shuts his eyes. "I mean, I worked hard this morning. I deserve a reward."

I lean over to kiss him on the forehead. "That you do, but we have a lot to do. I'll wake you after my shower."

"Damn, a shower with you sounds nice."

"You have the rest of your life to take a shower with me." I kiss him one more time.

"That I do. I'm one lucky bastard." He winks and shuts his eyes.

I run my hand down Annabelle's back. She sighs and tightens her grip on her daddy. Yeah, neither one of us wants to lose this man.

CHAPTER 7

"My body thanks you."

Cory

I blink to make sure what I'm seeing is real. The girl I talked to on the bus last night is climbing over the wall to the pool area but ends up in the bushes. I stop the treadmill to help her, but one of the employees opens the gate.

They have a conversation, and he allows her to stay even though it clearly says the pool is closed. *I'd do the same, buddy.* Watching her body sink into the pool, I decide to start the treadmill back up and admire her while I finish my workout.

She's definitely not a leisure swimmer. She must've competed at some point in her life. After forty-five minutes of me telling myself to leave well enough alone, that I'm here for a wedding and then I'm going back to start my season soon, I still find myself stopping the treadmill and walking out to the pool area.

When she reaches the end of the pool, she stops, presumably seeing my shadow.

"I see you used those horrible looks of yours to score an early dip in the pool?" I chuckle.

She shakes her head, pulling her goggles off completely. I squat so we're closer to eye level. Her eyes follow the beads of sweat dripping down my tattooed chest, glistening on my warm brown skin. I run a towel over my face, and her vision snaps up to my eyes again.

"You have no idea what I did to get in here early," she says, and I teeter back and forth about whether to tell her that I witnessed it.

I glance at the windows in front of the treadmills and back down at her. "Why don't you tell me over breakfast?"

"Breakfast?"

"You do eat, right?" My calves are cramping since all my body weight is on the balls of my feet.

"Yes, I eat, but..."

"Are you not finished with your swim? I thought maybe you might be since you've been out here for forty-five minutes."

A smile tilts the corners of her kissable lips. "Were you spying on me?" She looks over her shoulder at that wall of windows in the workout area.

"Technically, I was running on a treadmill. Just when I was about to call it quits and enjoy my vacation, you came into view. Somehow, watching you swim held my interest. My body thanks you." I wink.

Her hand floats under the water to her belly and I hope it's to calm the flips of her stomach, because mine is reacting the same way.

"How did I not think the people in there would see me?" She grabs the lane separator to stay afloat.

"Don't worry, it's me, you, and an elderly gentleman who's in better shape than both of us combined."

She smiles that warm, inviting grin that pulled me in on the bus.

"So... breakfast?" I arch an eyebrow.

"Don't you have wedding duties to attend to?"

I blanch. "Fuck no. Er... sorry, I mean, no. I'm not a groomsman."

"I thought maybe you were the groom after the greeting you got last night."

I fall to my ass on the cement and rest my forearms on my knees. "Is that a no to breakfast?"

She tilts her head as if she doesn't understand.

"You keep asking me questions we could discuss over an omelet, French toast, fresh fruit..."

She holds up her finger. "One more question, and then I'll give you my answer."

I nod. "My name? Cory. Cory Freeman."

She shakes her head. "The girl from last night. Do you have a girlfriend, Cory Freeman?"

I squint, trying to remember what she could be referring to. The girl who jumped into my arms. I didn't even know her. She was some groupie the guys were hanging around with at the bar. I set her down on her feet immediately afterward and walked away.

"No." I laugh. "She's a friend."

"Friend?" She tilts her head as if she doesn't believe me.

"I'm single..." I wait for her to fill in her name, but she doesn't.

"The word friend can have a lot of different meanings to different people." She leans over the concrete edge of the pool and my gaze dips to her cleavage in the one-piece suit, but I bounce my gaze back to hers quickly.

"None that would make us sharing a meal wrong."

She stares blankly at me.

I lean closer and lower my voice. "I went to bed about twenty minutes after we arrived... alone."

She appears to contemplate something for a long time, and I ready myself for her to decline my invitation.

"Okay. Let's do breakfast." She pulls herself out of the pool so she's standing on the edge.

I stand, and my eyes widen when we're both at full height and her breathing hitches as though she just realized something.

"I have one question though." I raise my finger. "My mom wouldn't approve if I had breakfast with a strange woman."

She giggles and shakes her head.

"What's your name?"

"Ande," she says with a smile.

"Andy?" I clarify.

"Like the small chocolate mints. A-N-D-E."

She's definitely sweet as candy.

I stick out my hand and lick my bottom lip. "Pleasure to meet you, Ande."

She shakes my hand while water drips off her skin onto the concrete. "Pleasure, Cory."

As we walk back inside the resort, I throw on the T-shirt that was tucked into the waistband of my shorts. Ande puts on a swim cover-up. Unfortunate for me.

"Buffet or sit down?" I ask when we approach the two restaurants that are open in the all-inclusive resort.

"Let's do buffet," she says. "More options."

"You like having options?" I ask, my hand landing on the small of her back as we walk. "And you were worried *I* wasn't single."

She opens her mouth, but I lead her with the warmth of my hand toward the buffet restaurant's hostess stand.

"Two please," Ande says.

"Can we be on the patio facing the water and under an umbrella, please?" I lean in to make my request, and for a second, Ande leans in closer to me.

The hostess's eyes light up and I watch her gaze fall down my body before popping back up. She's probably close to my age, midtwenties or younger. "Yes. For sure. Um... just give me a moment."

"Thanks," I say, and we walk to the side of the waiting area for her to return.

"I have a feeling you always get what you want," Ande teases.

I shrug. "Lately," I mumble, without adding anything else.

The guys kept razzing me about taking the shuttle bus to the resort and not grabbing a cab or have a car waiting, but that's not me. I didn't grow up with the kind of money I'm making right now, and hiring a car seems like a waste when there's already a free shuttle bus.

The hostess returns moments later and grabs two sets of silverware wrapped in napkins. "Follow me."

We follow her to the table, and when we arrive, I pull out Ande's chair and slide it back in after she's seated.

"Thank you," she says softly.

"Now you know three things about me. My name is Cory, I'm a gentleman, and I'm..." I sit down, leaning in closer. "Single," I whisper and wink.

She stares at me for a moment, and I revel in the lust that fills her eyes.

I clear my throat before I try to kiss her. "Yet all I know about you is that you like options, you have two friends with you on this trip, and I'd certainly lose if I tried to swim against you."

She giggles as the busboy fills our water goblets. Then a waiter comes by to introduce himself and tell us to help ourselves to the buffet. I stand before Ande, and we walk over to the buffet area. It's early, so the few guests who are here remain quiet and subdued as though they're not fully awake yet.

After we've each grabbed our food, I rejoin her at the table, placing two plates down in front of me. An omelet with egg whites and vegetables with a side of cantaloupe, grapes, and berries. The second plate has a big waffle with melted butter puddled into every crevice and a syrup cup overflowing on the side. She's got yogurt and fresh fruit.

"Do you work out just to eat?" she asks, her eyes as big as my waffle.

I chuckle, putting my napkin on my lap and pulling out my silverware. "I eat this." I point at the omelet and fruit. "So I can eat that," I say, pointing my fork at the waffle.

"Seems like a pretty simple mantra." She chuckles.

"Yeah." I nod, cutting my omelet with the side of my fork. "This is off—" I abruptly stop, just as I did on the bus. "I'm a growing boy." I pat my flat stomach while chewing a mouthful of egg and mushroom.

When I first joined the league, the guys warned me about the girls who chase hockey players. And even though I don't think Ande is a puck bunny, I want her to like me for me and not because I'm a Florida Fury hockey player.

"So, Ande, tell me about yourself." I pick up my juice and gulp down half of it in one swallow.

She shrugs. "Not much to say. I live in Salt Lake City."

I pause from eating when she doesn't continue. "And?"

"Do you want me to spout off some profile from a dating app?"

I lean back, laughing, and wipe my mouth.

"I'm twenty-five. Like I said, I live in Salt Lake City. I'm a graphic designer for a large firm, but I'm the newbie, so don't ask whether I've worked with anyone well known. I haven't. And you met my two best friends—Sophie and Brit. We're here on a girls' trip."

I nod. "Girls' trip? This an annual thing, or is there a specific reason?"

She chokes on her coffee. "What?"

"Is it someone's birthday or something?"

"Oh." She inhales deeply. "No. Nothing like that."

I lower my fork and stretch out in the seat because this chair is confining as hell for my height. "You're hiding something."

"No." She sips her coffee, taking care not to choke this time.

"I can tell. You're dodging eye contact." I point at her.

She blushes, and it's a great look on her.

"It's a 'better off without him' trip," she admits.

I nod because I'd kind of assumed it was something like that. But now for the real truth. "Your friend Sophie, the one who drank too much?"

She shakes her head.

"The one who probably does spreadsheets for fun... Brit?"

"You have a good memory, since I never introduced you." She spoons her yogurt.

"What can I say, that's another tidbit of information about myself. I'm observant."

"And yet you didn't know if you were on the right bus?" She looks at me over the rim of her coffee mug.

"So it's for you." I finish my juice and push the empty plate aside, sliding the waffle in front of me.

That means if something were to happen between us, it'd not only be a vacation fling, but a rebound.

"What's for me?"

"The 'forget the asshole' trip."

A tinge of embarrassment colors her cheeks. "It's a 'better off without him' trip."

I cock my head. "Is there a difference?"

She looks down at her plate.

"All right, give me the deets?"

She's quiet and avoids looking at me. She owes me nothing if she chooses not to share, but I'm not ready to give up yet.

"How long were you together? When did you break up?" I wave my hand to encourage her to talk.

"Why is it so important?"

I decide to admit something to her. "You clearly didn't realize I asked you about the bus as an excuse to talk to you. I need to know what I'm up against."

CHAPTER 8

Ande

A huge shiver runs up my spine. While he continues to eat his waffle as though he doesn't mind if I ruin our meal talking about my ex, my stomach clenches, not wanting to live in that bubble of scorned girlfriend. I want to get back to the girl I used to be. The one who believed in happily ever afters and destiny. For a moment, I was back to being her while sitting at this table with a gorgeous man who could have his pick of any woman in this resort.

"We met our senior year of college. We dated for almost four years until six months ago, when I caught him with someone else." I get all the basic details out without sounding angry or tearing up. I deserve a pat on the back.

He shakes his head and swallows. "Sorry."

My gaze falls to the ocean, spotting a few couples walking hand in hand as the sun travels farther up into the sky, the waves rolling to a slow tumble by their ankles. A woman squeals when a man pretends to push her in.

"You miss him?" he asks, his voice low.

I shake my head. "No."

An urge falls over me to tell him it's not Jackass I miss. It's me, the person I used to be. The one who thought people came into my life for a reason.

"Hmm…" He pushes his plate away and wipes his mouth before downing the entire bottle of water in front of him. "I'm not sure I believe you."

He waits as though he's aware I'm holding something back. How can a man I don't know see the fear gripping my insides? I open my mouth to tell him. He's a stranger and when we leave here, he'll quickly forget about the broken girl he flirted with over breakfast. But a crowd of men head in our direction, making a lot of noise, with overfilled plates in their hands.

"Freeman!" one of them says, taking a chair at the table before he even realizes I'm sitting here.

Cory pulls at his neck and catches my eye. "What's up, Train?"

I scrunch my eyebrows at the name.

"Get away from Jet and his girl." Another guy, who looks a little older than the rest, smacks the guy who's already digging into his plate across the head.

"Thanks, Zeus," Cory says and the longer-haired god nods and smiles at me.

The difference from last night is there aren't any girls with the group.

"I should go." I push my hands on the arms of the patio chair to stand.

"Wait. I'll walk you back." Cory stands. As we tuck our chairs back in, he pulls out a money clip and leaves a nice tip on the table. "See yah, Train."

"Sure thing," he mumbles over a muffin while forking a piece of fruit. Once he swallows, his gaze fixates on me. "You have a nice day. I'll be at the pool later. I'll be the stud with all the ladies, but there's always room for one more."

"Fuck off," Cory says and shakes his head.

We're about to step off the patio to the walkway leading to the villas when the Zeus guy calls to Cory, "Jet, we've got volleyball in an hour. I grabbed your sorry ass, so you better be there and ready to win!"

Cory waves and nods.

We pass the attendants adding towels to the lounge chairs and the bartender stocking the swim bar. I have to wonder what kind of wedding trip this is that people get up this early.

"What's with the names, Jet?" I push my shoulder against his, and he fumbles to catch his footing as if he was lost in thought. He seems different since the guys interrupted us.

"Ah." He pulls at his neck again. "You know guys. You do one stupid thing and you're branded for life."

"I guess. I've never had a nickname." I shrug, stopping at the path to the villa I'm staying in.

"No? Pet name?"

"Not anything past babe or sweetie or some other cliché."

He taps his finger against his full lips, and again the sight of his hand draws me in. What is it about them? Except this time, I'm wondering what our hands would look like together, our fingers interlaced. The contrast of his rich complexion and my fair skin. Now I'm imagining what our naked bodies would look like gliding and sliding along one another.

"I might have to change that for you."

His deep timbre draws me from my thoughts.

As if he was wondering the same thing as me, he reaches for my hand, his fingers grazing mine until I link one finger with his. I've never been with anyone as forward as Cory, and it's nice not to second-guess what he's thinking.

"I have a lot of obligations this weekend, but I want to see you," he says. "Will you and your friends come down to the beach today? I have the rehearsal dinner tonight and it's on a Catamaran. Since it's a relatively small wedding, they've invited everyone along. I'm not sure when I'll be back, but..."

He's so forward, but still wanting me to meet him halfway. It's perfect, really.

I dig inside my bag and grab my phone, then I unlock it and hand it to him. "Add your number in there. Text me and we'll see."

Our fingers brush as he takes the phone, then his thumbs make quick work of his task. "I'm not usually like this, but..." He steps closer, sliding my phone into the small slit of my bag. He raises his hand and I watch his tongue slide out and wet his lips while he stares at my own lips, his eyelids heavy. "Is this too much too soon?"

I shake my head without even thinking. It's as if my libido has short-circuited the pathway from my brain to my mouth and taken over control.

He smiles, and his perfect teeth appear with the wideness of his grin. It's way too much for a girl like me to handle. His lips move closer, and I inhale one last breath and release it with the hope that by the time this is over, I'll be starved for oxygen.

His long fingers grip the back of my hair, positioning my head to the perfect angle for him to bend down to meet me.

"ANDE!"

I squeeze my eyes shut at the sound of Brit's yelling.

Cory shakes his head and peers over my shoulder. He steps back, his hand sliding down my arm. "Hmm... tell your friend to put me on your to-do list today." He squeezes my hand once and walks back down the path. "Morning, Brit." He waves.

I laugh and turn toward my friend, who just cock-blocked me.

CHAPTER 9

Warner

*I*t's the night of the rehearsal dinner. I only know that because I watched them all leave earlier. Other than Imogen leaving with them, it was like a rush of fresh air knowing I won't be running into Ford for at least a few hours.

Casen, Grey, Nala, and I decide to go to the upscale Japanese steak house restaurant at the resort. After we eat, Casen and I head to the outdoor bar, and I'm happy that Nala and Grey go to check out the shops in the resort.

"Seriously, Casen?" I say since it's the first time I've had him alone.

"Are you talking about the fact that Jacobs's wedding is here?" He sips his beer. "Classic."

"No, I'm talking about the fact that you hooked me up with a girl who thinks she's the lion from *The Lion King*."

He laughs even harder. "No, she doesn't. She's way into you, by the way."

"She's into the fact that I'm a professional hockey player."

Casen is smarter than this. He knows Grey and Nala are the type of women who only want to be with us because we're hockey players. Does Nala like me? Probably. But I bet if I continued this dating thing, and we became a couple, she'd be telling everyone and their third cousin that I play hockey professionally. She'd be volunteering tickets to games, asking for special reservations at restaurants. All of which I'm not into.

As I'm imagining the thought, a loud roar of laughter and voices rings throughout the dark night sky. I don't have to look to know Ford and his entourage are coming around the bend of the resort into the open bar area. My chest squeezes for a second because at one point, I thought I'd be right alongside him for this milestone in his life.

"Looks like the quiet is over," Casen says.

My gaze finds Imogen first. She's laughing at something the guy next to her said. I don't know the guy and I'm assuming he's someone's plus-one. But he definitely likes her if his body language is any indication. My inner beast breaks through from just seeing another man making her laugh the way I used to.

I take a pull from my beer. "I should call it a night."

"No way." Casen sits up straighter and turns to the group. He's familiar with them. Played with Kane for a while in Colorado. "Congrats, Richie!" He raises his drink. "Give them a round on me," he tells the bartender, who nods.

"Thanks, Casen. One day you might find yourself as lucky as me." Ford puts his arm around Lena's waist and kisses her temple.

"I can only hope," he says back and turns to me. "Not. What are the odds?"

"Odds of what?" I ask, ignoring Ford's eyes piercing into my skull every time he turns around. So far, we've been nice to one another when passing at the resort—if nice means pretending the other doesn't exist.

"Odds they actually make it. This industry isn't made for marriage."

Casen isn't ready to settle down and maybe he never will be, but he's always sharing his opinion on how no one in the industry should marry. It only ends in divorce. I've seen plenty of hockey players make it work, with the result being cute kids and happy parents. I don't agree with Casen's line of thinking.

I do, however, know it takes someone special to marry a professional athlete. They have to be secure with themselves and have their own thing going for them. But it's also the player's job to make sure they have nothing to worry about. Like call them after the game and don't be out at some club, getting drunk and picking up women.

"Honestly, as much as Ford and I don't see eye to eye, I'd bet the house she's the one."

"What? You serious?"

I look over his shoulder. Lena's got Annabelle in her arms and she's dancing to the music. My gaze shifts to Ford, who's talking to his dad, but his eyes are only on his fiancée and his daughter. "Yeah, they'll make it."

Years ago, I might've said no because Ford wasn't ready to settle down, but something obviously changed in his life and the bastard got what I've always wanted. A family of my own. A family to give everything to. I should be jealous, but truth is, I'm envious. There's no anger that I don't have the same, because I could've. I messed that up myself and I'm the only one to blame.

Casen scoffs. "You're delusional."

Ford leaves his dad and whispers something to Lena. The two of them tell their guests something and walk toward the villas with Annabelle.

I immediately think that this is my time to get to Imogen, but I know it's not a smart idea. Still, I need her to understand how much I regret everything that happened between us.

"Warner!" Nala uses her usual high decibel voice to get my attention.

Why can't she wait until she's closer before calling my name? There's no reason to shout it over all these people except for the fact that she wants everyone to know she's with me.

"What's this with Grey then?" I ask Casen before the girls make it over to us.

He shrugs, opening his arm to welcome her to his side. "Fun. I do enjoy lazy mornings in bed." He winks, then slides over, allowing Grey to sit next to him. "How were the shops?"

"It was okay."

"I found the cutest purse, but it's way too expensive." Nala pretends to pout like a toddler.

"That sucks." I down another gulp of my beer.

She cuddles up next to me, putting her cheek on my shoulder, and her finger travels down my chest. "You could buy it for me."

My gaze goes to Casen, who's trying to hide his grin. Damn him.

Wanting to look anywhere but at Nala, my gaze travels the room and spots Imogen in the corner with that douche she was walking with earlier. Seriously, the guy is wearing boat shoes. I know that's the type she's used to since her family is rich as fuck, but she doesn't like guys like that. She likes guys like me. Rough around the edges, with hidden hearts of gold.

She looks up while stirring her drink with the little straw. Our eyes lock until she looks to my side and quickly turns back to the douche.

My heart squeezes painfully. God, I'd do about anything to talk to her right now.

Her head falls back, and the guy seems surprised she's laughing, which tells me she's putting on an act for me. Is she really gonna do that? But sure enough, her hand goes to his knee, and the douche slides closer.

My inner beast rises up once again, clawing at the inside of my chest. I intently watch her, but it feels as if she's almost getting off on having my eyes on her. Like she wants her revenge and is using this opportunity to get it.

She stands and I pray like hell she's going to the bathroom because I can feign having to take a piss too. But instead she takes his hand. My jaw clenches as I watch her take him over to the shuffleboard game.

"We should play," I say without thinking of the repercussions.

"Play what?" Nala asks.

"No, you shouldn't," Casen chimes in.

"Shuffleboard?" I stand and hold my hand out to Nala.

"You're asking to get your ass kicked," Casen murmurs around his beer.

"Then come have my back."

He stands and shakes his head, mumbling about what a jackass I am. Ignoring him, I lead Nala over to the shuffleboard.

"Care if we join you?" I ask the douche. "She's been dying to play." I thumb toward an oblivious Nala who is dancing in place to the music.

Imogen turns around. "Yes, we do care."

I finish my beer and set it on the table. "It'll be fun."

"It's better with couples, and this way I can show you how to play," the douche says to Imogen.

I narrow my eyes at her. "You don't know how to play?"

She sips her drink. "No. I don't."

I could call her out on her bullshit. The Jacobs have a shuffleboard in their billiards room. Her dad loves to play, and she's played since she was a young girl. Why would she lie?

"Nala hasn't either, so this should be fun." I look at Nala, who is now talking to the waitress about the flowers in the pots set around the patio area. "Nala!"

She peeks up like an obedient dog and runs over, abandoning the waitress. "Warner!" She looks at Imogen and the douche, putting out her hand. "Hi, I'm Nala."

"Imogen," she says with distaste and looking more at me than Nala.

"Eddie," the guy says and looks her up and down.

I'd offer him a trade if I thought Imogen would say yes. She'd probably knee me in the nuts.

"Let's go." I start the game, knowing my time is probably limited. My assumption is Ford and Lena went to put Annabelle to bed. I have no idea if they'll be back here at some point. For all I know, they went to leave Annabelle with his parents. "How about we do boys against one another, then girls, then the two winners play one another?"

That will surely taunt Imogen's competitive nature and I'll get to play with her in the final round.

"I don't know. We were going to take a walk on the beach," Eddie says, looking at Imogen.

My hands fist at my sides.

"We're in," she says without even looking at Eddie.

"Great. You can go first, Eddie." I motion to the table.

Eddie's and my game goes as predicted. I win because I played on the Jacobs' shuffleboard table plenty of times.

Nala is so busy dancing and drinking that she's no threat

to Imogen, which leaves Imogen and me going head to head.

Nala and Eddie sit at the table nearby with a fresh round of drinks. Ford still hasn't reappeared, and by now Imogen seems almost civil to me.

"Ladies first," I say, winking.

We both sidle up on the same side of the table as she says, "I can't believe you swindled this. You're lucky Ford's not here."

She shoots, then we switch spots.

"Come to my room tonight. Let's talk." I hit her disc off the board, and she can't get back in position soon enough. I do love competitive Imogen. Such a turn-on.

She blanches. "You're kidding, right? Why would I do that?" She has just the right touch and takes the lead.

"Because you know we have unfinished business. Otherwise, what happened at Ford's house, wouldn't have. I'm not looking for a hookup. I'm looking to apologize and explain my side of things." I shoot and get close, but she's still winning.

We switch spots again.

"It's over between us. It's been years, Warner. Why now?"

"I'll answer you tonight. Just come to my room. I'm in villa four, room four twenty-three."

She shakes her head and throws another one that knocks my closest disc off the board. "I can't. There's nothing between us anymore. I think you said all you had to say way back when." She looks at the board and back at me. "I win, which means I get what I want, and that's for you to leave me alone."

I glance at Nala and Eddie, who are facing the ocean and involved in their own conversation. I step closer to Imogen. "I don't believe you, Gen."

Her head tilts up to look at me. "Believe it. We were over that day."

I stare at her for I have no idea how long, taking in the hurt and mistrust in her eyes. But there's still a spark there too.

"You son of a bitch!" Ford's voice comes from somewhere behind me.

A touch of sadness overtakes Imogen's beautiful blue eyes before she blinks it away and steps back as though she's waiting for her brother to slide between us.

I hold up my hands. "We were just talking, and I'm leaving."

Ford shoves me, and I knock into a waitress with a tray of drinks, and the glasses crash to the floor.

Kane quickly intercepts. "Stop it. Langley, go to your room."

"You can't always be her protector," I say to Ford. "It's her life, not yours."

"Not as long as there's blood in my veins. You'll never touch her again." His fists clench.

I ignore him and stare at Imogen while weaving through the room and out onto the beach.

One thing I really need to figure out is if fighting for Imogen is worth it in the end, because right now, everything is against me. But I want nothing more than her, so where does that leave me?

Chapter 10

"Can I see if my expectations have been met?"

Cory

The wedding isn't until sunset, so we have the entire day to mess around. At least those of us who aren't in the wedding.

I walk down to the beach and find Ande talking to the cabana rental guy.

"Is there a problem?" I ask.

The attendant looks at me, and his eyes widen because I'm one of the Florida Fury guys. Or maybe because I'm six-three.

"All the cabanas are booked up, but Brit thought one came with the villa." Ande looks back at the attendant. "It might not seem like it, but I'm saving you if you get me a cabana before my friend shows up."

I laugh and mumble, "Truth."

"Jet!" Zeus yells, spinning a volleyball on his pointer finger over by the nets.

I hold up my finger, then dig my credit card from my string backpack. "Surely you can find something for the lady. Bill it to my room."

"Of course, Mr. Freeman."

"No." Ande's hand covers my own. "You can't do that."

I slide my hand out from hers, turn around, and rest my back against the counter the employee is behind.

"Maybe I have my own reasons for needing a cabana." I tap my credit card against my lips. I'm not usually this bold, but I really want Ande.

"Like?" she asks.

"Truth?"

"Always."

"It might scare you." My gaze locks with hers and her eyes hold mine.

"Try me."

Although I've never had one, between all the sexual energy on just a bus ride, a breakfast, and now this, I'm starting to understand one-night stands.

I lean forward, swiping her hair over her shoulder, and lower my voice. "If your friends get distracted by my friends, then we have the cabana all to ourselves."

The best blush washes over her cheeks as if she's been in the sun too long.

"Damn, girl, I love that look on you. I want to see that flush cover your entire body."

She closes her eyes for a moment and breathes deeply.

"So..." I walk around her until her back presses against my front and I slide my card across the ledge of the counter. "I'll cover the cabana," I whisper in her ear.

Goose bumps erupt on her arms. My lips are so close to her ear, and she arches her back into me. Just as I'm about to ask the attendant for that cabana right now, her friends appear. Even with each of them having cover-ups on, my teammates' gazes follow their movements.

"Seriously, you two are always in a compromising position." Brit rolls her eyes, but her smile says she doesn't truly care.

"Another thing you should know about me—I'm a

matchmaker extraordinaire," I say, leaving Ande and waving for Brit and Sophie to follow me.

I introduce Ande's friends to my friends.

Sophie and Brit shed their cover-ups and toss them by their bags. Brit starts bending and stretching. I guess she's playing volleyball. Sophie sits on the brick ledge and Train heads right over, leaning his hip on the ledge with his arms crossed while he chats her up.

I leave the volleyball court, go back toward Ande, and the attendant tells me which cabana number we have. "It's all set. Do you want to play with us?"

We walk away from the attendant.

"Volleyball?" she asks.

I chuckle. "We can't make our getaway just yet."

"Says who?"

My eyes widen. "Here I thought I'd have to convince you."

She leans forward. "Convince me of what?"

"To play some tonsil hockey in the cabana."

Her eyes look like a drug addict's who just got offered cocaine. Demanding and wanting whatever I'll give her.

"No convincing needed, but I'll play first," she says, tossing her bag next to her friends' and lifting the hem of her cover-up over her body.

"Shit," I murmur. She's got a body I want to worship.

"You look smokin'," Sophie calls.

Although Train doesn't say anything, his eyes are eating Ande up.

My jaw clenches. "Fuck, Train, stop gawking."

He holds up his burly hands. "You can't be serious."

"As a fucking heart attack. If your tongue doesn't get back inside your mouth, it's on."

Train laughs. "You're full of shit." But Train does return

his focus to Sophie, who tells him she's not really into guys who look at her friends with fuck-me eyes.

My hand falls to Ande's lower back and this time it's skin on skin. "I changed my mind. Cabana it is."

She giggles. "You saw me in a swimsuit this morning."

I guffaw. "You're kidding, right? This has about eighty percent less fabric to it."

"I'm going to be honest, I'm not really sorry."

My gaze rolls over her body like warm honey and her nipples stiffen, poking through the fabric. "Don't be. Not one bit."

She laughs as Zeus huddles everyone together, dividing Ande and Brit so there's one girl on each team. I get Brit and Zeus while Ande's on the other team with Tweetie and one of the other guys who is here for the wedding. I think he's Ford's cousin or something. I don't know his name because we haven't spoken yet. I grumble about the way the teams have been split, but don't argue.

Ande still doesn't know I play professional hockey and I know for sure she's wondering why all these men have nick-names. She's already asked about mine.

On the first play, Ande jumps to get the ball, but Sham-rock reaches it first, spiking it. The ball hits my head since I'm stunned from watching her tits bounce up and down.

"I'm going to call myself out right now. I just can't with her across from me." I raise my hand like we're in school and I'm asking permission to be excused. Without another word, I dip under the net to her side and take her hand. "We're going for a swim."

She giggles and trails along behind me as I eat up the distance between us and the pool. We're barely submerged in the pool before I wrap my arm around her waist and bend for her to straddle me in the water.

"Is this okay?" I ask, walking us over to where the pool gets deeper.

She nods, biting her lip. The feel of her soft curves against my hard body is divine.

"I need you to know something before we go any further."

She stiffens in my arms. That asshole sure messed her up. "You're not single?"

I laugh quietly. "No, I'm single. Man, that chump did a number, huh?"

"Okay, that's all I need to know. You don't owe me any other explanation. This is just a vacation fling. You don't have to bare your soul."

Hmm... I've heard that before and usually it's true, but with Ande, I'm not sure I believe her. I study her for a long time. "Right. Yeah."

She wraps her arms around my neck, the water cooling off my skin, but I'm growing harder by the minute with her so close. "Where were we then?"

I kiss the hollow of her neck. "Here?"

"That's a good start." She grinds along my hard length.

"I'm not really into the public thing. Want to disappear to the cabana, or can I entice you to my room?" My voice turns gravelly from the want that's eating me up.

This is moving faster than I thought, but I want this. I want to feel her under me. See what gets her off and master it.

"Your room."

"Thank fuck."

She dislodges from me, and I fix myself so that my bathing suit isn't tented with a huge hard-on as we emerge from the water. We each grab our bags while Brit and Zeus are chest to chest, arguing about a call. Sophie and Train are busy getting drinks, so no one really notices us sneaking off.

"What a waste of money for the cabana," Ande says.

I shrug, linking my hand with hers. "It's fine. I'd rather have you in my room anyway."

We walk past her villa and up the pathway leading to my room.

We climb two floors and I pause at my door with my key card out. "You can change your mind. There's no rush."

She places her hand over mine and swipes the key card. The light goes from red to green.

I open the door, and she walks into my oceanfront room with a king-size bed, small sitting area, and a balcony. Walking the length of my room, she drops her bag on the couch and wraps her arms around herself.

I come up behind Ande and wrap my arms around her waist, clasping my hands at her stomach. "You sure?"

She nods and turns around in my arms. "I know I said we didn't have to tell each other anything, but you should know that I've never done this."

"You're a virgin?" I smirk.

She lightly smacks my chest. "I've never had sex with someone I barely know."

I rest my forehead against hers. "I've never done this either."

"Somehow I doubt that."

I blow out a breath. "I've never felt so connected to someone I barely know. Felt this pull. Like there's something here to be discovered."

"After only a couple days?"

I frown, assuming she doesn't believe me. "I guess what I'm trying to say is..." My fingers run up and down her spine.

"I'm a private person. I don't tend to let anyone in, not even just for one night. I'm guarded."

Can I really trust her? She could snap a picture and it'd be all over social media by day's end.

"I know you've been hurt, and I've been burned a few times myself, but since you trust me enough to tell me you've never had a one-night stand, I want to tell you... my friends at the beach. Zeus, Train, and them..." I splay my hand on her back, pulling her flush against me.

"Go on."

"They're my friends, that's true, but they're also my teammates. I play for the Florida Fury."

She tilts her head a bit. "Oh. Is that football?"

I chuckle, and my fingers slide a stray lock of hair behind her ear. "No. Professional hockey."

Relief floods me that she hasn't been pretending. She really has no idea who my teammates and I are.

"I'm going to be honest, I wouldn't have known if you didn't say anything." She cringes as if I should be insulted. Quite the opposite.

"Well, I want you to know. It's why I'm guarded. Women use professional athletes. They trick us into trying to get pregnant. I'm one of the few black hockey players in the pros. In all actuality, I'm mixed race because my mom is white and my dad is black, but society views me as a black man because of the color of my skin. I feel responsible to be a good role model for kids and to let the black kids out there know their dream is possible. So I guess this is my confession to you that I don't usually do this either."

She steps closer to me, her breasts smashing against my chest. "Your secret is safe with me."

She stands on her tiptoes to kiss me, but I lower my head and my lips meet hers first. It doesn't take long for all the sexual energy that's been swirling around us to take control. I circle us without breaking the kiss, the backs of her knees hitting the bed. My fingers trail up her back and tug at the strings of her bikini. I watch in awe as the two triangles fall, revealing a set of perfect breasts.

I suck in a breath. "I've been dying to do that all morning, and damn, it's lived up to every expectation I had."

"Can I see if my expectations have been met?" She glides one finger down my chiseled abs and cups my hard length in her palm.

I slide my swimming trunks down to my ankles, baring myself to her. "Well?"

She shoves down her swim bottoms and crawls up the bed. "You'll do."

Ande giggles as I tackle her to the bed, sucking one of her breasts into my mouth. I pin her to the plush hotel mattress and prove to her how much I want her by bringing her to orgasm—three times.

After we're spent and enjoying our postcoital bliss, Zeus calls and tells me that I need to help out with something for the wedding. Reluctantly, I get dressed and ready to go.

I toss my key card to Ande. "I'll text you when I'm on my way back and you can meet me here so we can do more of that."

She fiddles with the key card as I climb onto the bed to give her a chaste kiss goodbye before leaving.

Right before I reach the group, I hammer out a text to her.

Me: *Figured out your new nickname... Hat Trick*
Ande: *What?*
Me: *Look it up and you'll understand.*

CHAPTER 11

Jana

The wedding is beautiful, which isn't surprising. The Jacobs have more money than my dad. Maybe. Probably. Well, it doesn't matter. They both have more money than they know what to do with.

Lena made a beautiful bride, and Annabelle was the sweetest flower girl even though Ford's youngest sister, Morgan, carried her down the aisle. Of course, Ford was a handsome groom. No tears, but a huge smile on his face when Lena appeared with Ford's dad at the end of the aisle.

Now, we're seated at the tables for dinner. They haven't done assigned seating, which I'm not really a fan of. I love assigned seats as much as the smart kid likes to sit in the front of the classroom.

The chair next to me gets pulled out and a large body sits down. I look over to see Kane there.

"You look beautiful," he says and takes a sip of his water.

"I don't have to sit next to you tonight. I did last night, remember?" I pick up my wineglass.

"Don't act like you don't like my company. It's not really working." He stops a waiter and orders himself a scotch.

I groan. My father's drink.

"Is there a problem?" Kane asks.

"I knew you were old. I just didn't realize you were an old man who drinks scotch."

He chuckles. "First of all, I don't think scotch is an old man's drink. Second, you want to order me a drink? Have at it." He leans back in his chair and splays his arms across the back of my seat.

The man is ridiculously sexy, and he knows it.

"Fine. I'll order you a drink."

"Go for it." He gestures to the returning waiter.

The waiter brings Kane's scotch, and I take it. "Actually, Mr. Burrows would like a Sex on the Beach." I twirl the scotch glass in my hand and down the contents in one gulp.

As the waiter leaves, Kane watches me so intently, there's a stirring in my lady parts. If I don't watch myself, I'm going to get in trouble here.

"I'd like sex on the beach, but not the drink." Kane's whiskey eyes eat me up.

I turn toward him, and since everyone is still mingling from cocktail hour, no one else is at our table. "Are you propositioning me?"

He laughs. "Me? Propositioning the boss's daughter? That'd be crazy."

I nod slowly. "It would be."

"That's why I'm not doing it."

"Good. Because I don't do hockey players." I drink some more of my wine. I'm lying to myself as much as I am him.

"Can I ask you a question then?" He leans in a bit.

"Sure. What?"

"Why the front? Why give me this bitchy side of yourself?"

My mouth drops open. "I'm not being a bitch."

"I said you're giving me a bitchy side of yourself. Those are two very different things."

A peachy-pink drink with an umbrella is set in front of Kane by the waiter.

"Way to not be embarrassed to order what you want." Cory Freeman smacks Kane's back. I didn't even notice him approach. He bends down and looks around quickly. "You think anyone would notice if I left?"

"The girl from the beach?" I ask our new rookie. "It's your business, but you might want to be careful. There are cameras on every phone and you two were pretty cozy out there."

"Who cares what the people on social media say? You're single and able to screw whoever you want. And no one is going to notice you're gone. Go be with your vacation fling," Kane tells Cory.

"Thanks." He smiles, then heads out before dinner is even served.

"Lucky bastard," Kane mumbles.

"What are you going on about?" I raise my glass and the waitress with the wine bottle comes over and fills it.

"He's going to go fuck all night."

"Doubtful. Once, maybe twice." I sip my wine.

"Not me. I'd last all night long."

My thighs clench together, but I play it as though I'm unfazed by this man. "Whatever. Men and their lies."

"I can prove it."

I turn completely toward him and narrow my eyes. "It really sounds like you want to take me to your room, Zeus." I don't know why I'm egging him on. This is a bad idea.

He shakes his head. "Don't call me that. I'm only Kane to you."

"Figured you want all the women to think of you as a god." I arch an eyebrow.

"To you, I'm just Kane."

"Aren't you bossy?"

"Come on, Jana. Let's stop playing games. The minute I walked into that boardroom, the sexual tension was alive between us and it was suffocating."

I shake my head. "We're at a wedding. Everyone gets this way at weddings. Ever wonder how many one-night stands happen at weddings?"

"One in five." Imogen sits down next to me.

"What?" I ask, looking over at her.

"I looked it up once. I'm not sure why or when. But that's a lot. Like, twenty percent of this group is five, but we'll up it to six because you need two to tango. We're a small group, so I don't think we'll hit the twenty percent, but let's say you two."

"Oh, we're not hooking up," I rush out.

Kane says nothing, his silent demeanor unnerving me.

"I mean, Cory is hooking up, but she's not a guest. Still that'd be four. Train has been hitting on Lena's friend pretty hard so... that would be five and six." She holds up six fingers and looks over at me.

"You need to find another two people, because we're not hooking up." I waggle my finger between Kane and me. The only thing worse than me hooking up with Kane would be everyone knowing about it. "Excuse me, I have to go to the bathroom."

I somehow manage to get through dinner. Luckily, Imogen and our friends distract me from the fact that Kane's thigh is touching mine. When the dancing starts, I opt to talk with Paisley until a slow song comes on and Maksim steals her from me.

A hand comes into my view. "Stop playing hard to get. Dance with me."

I look over at Kane. What is his deal? "No."

"It's just a dance, scaredy-cat," he says.

I don't want to play his childish games, but I'm also tired of Ford's parents giving me pitying looks since I've been sitting at this table all night, so I accept his hand.

"One dance."

"That's all it will take." He winks.

Kane leads me to the dance floor and pulls me in close. His large hand on the small of my back makes me feel feminine and petite, and when his thumb runs up and down where my dress dips and my skin is exposed, it sends a shiver through me.

I close my eyes because he smells delicious, and I love that I can wear heels and he's still inches taller than me. He's solid and makes me feel protected as he moves us around the dance floor.

I pull back to ask, "Have you taken dance lessons?"

He laughs. "My sister made me for her wedding. She and her husband are professional dancers and made their wedding party do a choreographed dance."

"Really?"

A chuckle leaves his lips. I just can't picture it.

He nods and rolls his eyes as if he's embarrassed.

"I like it. You're not just circling me around."

"I can dip you if you'd like," he says with a challenging look.

"Really?"

He moves me around and my feet barely catch up before he dips me and my back bends with the support of his hand. He pops me back up and twirls us again.

"Look at Zeus with all his moves," one of the players calls from a table.

"It's really impressive," I compliment him, my defensive wall crumbling.

Come on, Jana, your walls are stronger than that. So what if he can dance?

"Thanks."

Kane says nothing else but continues to move us across the dance floor as if we're gliding on ice. I attempt to follow, but I have nowhere near his talent. The song ends and I want another one to start so I can dance with him again, but it's a hip-hop song that, according to the DJ, Ford's sister Morgan requested.

"Come on a walk with me," Kane says, arms still wrapped around me.

I look up at him. "I can't. I'm the boss's daughter."

He glances right and left. "I don't see your dad here."

He has a point. My dad would have been here, but he already had a European vacation planned with my mom for the summer. Right now, I'm not sure if that's a blessing or a curse because of what I'm about to do.

I nod. "Okay."

His mouth widens in the most incredible smile, and I realize he has perfectly straight teeth, which is a rarity for a hockey player. Kane takes my hand. "Then let's go."

When we reach the sand, I slip off my heels and he rolls up his pants. What harm can a walk on the beach do?

CHAPTER 12

"See you soon, Hat Trick."

Andie

I laughed out loud after Googling "hat trick." Apparently it's when a player scores three goals in one game and it rarely happens.

As Cory requested, I met him in his room after the wedding last night. But we left for a walk on the beach, which turned into beach sex, which turned into the two of us showering in his room to remove about a million grains of sand from every square inch of our bodies.

He's heading back to Florida now and I join him in the lobby to say goodbye. It's hard to think we won't see each other again. I can't help but feel like there's a real possibility for us to be more than just a vacation fling, but the reality is that we live on different sides of the country.

"Maybe we can meet up. I start my season in a month. I could come to Salt Lake City in the meantime?" he says.

We both know that won't happen, having agreed last night that long distance won't work for us. I haven't told Cory, but I think doing a casual thing when we meet up from time to time would be a bad idea for me. I want a boyfriend. The irony is that he's the one who made me see that.

He tucks my hair behind my ear. "You'll hear rumors. But trust me, okay?"

I swallow him in a hug that doesn't nearly cover half of his body and hold him so tightly, I fear tears will spill. He owes me nothing.

"Let's go, Jet," Train says as he passes. "See you around, Candy Ande." He winks and heads to his Uber X, where some of his teammates already are.

"Hey, how come you took the bus instead of a private car on the way here?" I ask.

"Don't you know me at all?" Cory flashes me a smile. I guess he isn't interested in the fame and attention that comes with his profession. "Not to mention, if I had, I wouldn't have met you." He kisses me briefly, but it turns hot with his tongue sliding against mine. The hoots and hollers from his teammates rise out of the open windows of the Uber. "Think about coming to see me, okay?"

"Okay," I say, but we both know I won't.

"See you soon, Hat Trick," he says and shakes his head. "Damn, I need to come up with something better."

"Maybe next time," I say with a sad smile.

He nods. "Next time for sure."

I watch Cory walk to the Uber, Brit and Sophie linking their arms in mine as though they fear I'll crumble. He takes one last look at me before disappearing into the large black SUV, the dark tint of the windows hiding his movements from me. Is he looking at me until he can't see me anymore, or is he already in full razz mode with his teammates? I'll never know.

"You good?" Brit asks.

"It was just a vacation fling. I'm awesome," I lie and all three of us turn around.

As we walk inside, the woman behind the front desk flags us down and says they've been leaving messages for us. "Which of you is Miss Ande?"

"That's me."

"Here you go." She hands me some handwritten messages.

I go through them, all of them saying to call Sara, my boss, ASAP.

"Shit!" I look at both my friends. "My boss has been trying to get a hold of me. I haven't even looked at my phone since yesterday. I guess I—"

"Spent every minute with Cory?" Sophie grins.

We rush back to the room, and I dig through my bag until I find my phone. I press the button. "It's dead. How is it dead?"

"Um..." Sophie purses her lips as if she wants to say something.

I run to the two chargers Brit plugged in when we got here. Tapping my toes, I wait impatiently, bringing my nails to my mouth. "She knows I'm on vacation. I hope I didn't mess something up big time for a client."

Finally, the phone boots up, and my thumb hovers over the home button to unlock it. After what seems like a lifetime, I open it and spot a text from Cory first. Unable to resist, I open it. He snapped a picture of himself pouting. God, how can I already miss him?

I press the last voice mail and put it on speaker. It's Sara. "Where are you? I wanted to discuss this with you and not have to leave a voice mail, but I guess you really took this vacation thing to heart. I have news. The company is cutting back and closing the Salt Lake City office immediately. I managed to get a transfer to our Florida office, and I'd love for you to come there with me. You have a lot of potential. I know it's short notice but..." I listen as my friends frown, because if I take the job, it means I'll be moving away from them.

Florida is where Cory is. Is this some weird cosmic sign? Even if it is, all Cory and I discussed were casual meetups. He might be freaked out and think I'm a stalker if I move to his hometown.

Maybe our story is better left as a vacation fling. That will have to be enough.

CHAPTER 13

"As the princess wishes."

Kane

The buzzing of my phone wakes me.

As I roll over, my hand goes to the empty bed beside me. I peek one eye open, finding Jana putting her dress from last night back on.

"Where are you going? I booked an extra day to enjoy for myself. Thought maybe you'd stay too." I sit up on the bed and bring my knees up. I honestly thought we had something special and broke that barrier last night.

She walks over to the side of the bed. "Zip me up?" I do as she asks, then she's searching for earrings. "Don't pretend we didn't know what this was. We're both adults, Zeus."

"Why are you calling me that?" I ask between gritted teeth.

"Because it's your nickname."

She sits on the edge of the bed to put on her shoes. I crawl over and kiss her neck, allowing my hands to find the zipper I just zipped up.

She abruptly stands and I almost face-plant on the floor. "What the hell?"

"Come on. We're the twenty percent, right? The ones who hook up at a wedding. Now we go home and pretend it didn't happen." She grabs her clutch purse.

I blink a couple times because she's caught me off guard.

I thought we were on the same page—that this was the beginning of something, not the end.

"You think you can forget me?" I ask, leaning against the headboard with only a sheet over my lap.

Her gaze roams my body and I see the lust there. She's mustering all the willpower she can not to climb on my lap and let me wish her a good morning properly. But that wall she's so good at erecting is back in place and the woman who was begging me for more last night has disappeared. "See you in Florida, Zeus."

I climb out of the bed naked, and as she opens the door, I slam it shut. "Why are you denying whatever this is between us?"

She stares at the floor.

I put my finger under her chin, raising it so her eyes meet mine. "Why?"

"I'm not denying anything. Last night was great, but let's not pretend we didn't go into this with the same expectation." Her hand lands on the doorknob again. "Please open the door."

"I'm not sure when I was the guy you think was only interested in this for a one-night stand."

"You said it yourself. Sexual tension in the boardroom."

"Yeah, that doesn't mean I want to fuck and chuck you." That she would think that makes anger simmer under my calm exterior. When I like a woman, I like her, and I sure as hell don't sleep with a woman just to get off. I do it because I want to be with her. Because I see more than just a bed in our future. Yeah, sometimes it doesn't work out, but I'm not a womanizer.

"Well, then." Her back straightens and I wait for her bullshit. "I'm sorry, because that's all I wanted from you. Bye."

She opens the door and I hold it shut for a second, but I'm not an asshole. If she wants to leave, then fine.

"As the princess wishes." I step out of her way.

She huffs, opening the door and walking through. After the door shuts, I sit on the edge of the bed, wondering what the fuck just happened.

***

NOT ABOUT TO SPEND MY last day here sulking, I head to the pool area and plant myself on a lounge chair. Since the other guys are gone, I don't feel like I have to play volleyball instead of relaxing.

"I thought everyone left?"

I open one eye to see Warner standing over me.

I sit up straighter in the lounge chair. "I booked an extra day. I think everyone left or is leaving. Ford and Lena went on a honeymoon somewhere else."

"Phew," he says and sits next to me. "I can finally have one day of relaxation."

"You bring it upon yourself."

He huffs. "Yeah, I probably do. Can I talk to you? Like, about it? I don't want to put you in a bad situation, but I need some advice on what the hell to do. I think I'm burning down the broken bridge I'm trying to rebuild here."

I laugh, remembering Mr. Gerhardt and even Coach telling me to take on the role of mentor to the players. That I have a lot of expertise in the league and should help the others.

"Of course, shoot."

We end up going in the pool, ordering a few drinks at the swim-up bar, and Warner tells me everything. From him attending Ford's high school, to them playing hockey together, to his secret relationship with Imogen, to why Ford hates him and Imogen doesn't want anything to do with him. They have valid reasons, and this is a hard rebuild he's trying for.

"I still love her, Zeus. I don't think I ever stopped."

"Why did you wait so long then?"

It's the question everyone is going to ask him.

"I didn't think I deserved her. I thought she was better without me, but now that I'm face to face with her, all those feelings are rushing back. I feel like I'm on a kayak in the middle of the most dangerous river and I've never white water rafted before. But it hurts to see her and not be able to touch her."

I clap Warner on the shoulder. I feel bad for him. It has to suck. I'm still processing Jana's abrupt departure, but I'm older and wiser. And I sure as shit am not in love with her.

"If I were you, I'd just play it slow. Let her get to know you again."

As he's nodding and I think he's doing better, a shadow appears over us. We both look up to find Imogen in a sundress and sandals.

"Can I talk to you?" she asks Warner.

"Oh, I'm busy now, Imogen. Give me ten," I answer, pulling a smile from her.

"Sure," Warner says and climbs out of the pool without so much as a goodbye to me.

He grabs a towel, and she nods toward a table closer to the beach. I hope they can figure things out.

I swim back over to the bar and order a shot. I have my own shit to drown right now. I'm going back to Florida, and I'll have to see Jana all the damn time and forget how amazing she is in bed.

CHAPTER 14

Imogen

Someone should just chain me to a chair. Why am I engaging in conversation with Warner Langley right now? Because I feel like we need to clear the air. I just need to make it quick and say what I need to and get out.

It doesn't help that I find him at the pool, which means as I sit down across from him at the table, he's showing off those incredible abs and treasure trail.

"I should—" he begins, but I put my hand up to stop him.

"No. Please, may I?"

He nods for me to go ahead.

"I shouldn't have engaged in that petty game last night. I was jealous and…"

"Jealous?" he asks as if he has no clue what feelings I still hold for him.

But there's too much against us. Too much happened all those years ago. It's not something that can ever be taken back, even if I forgive him.

"Well, of course. But it doesn't change anything. What we had is over. I understand that now that we're both in Florida and you're playing for the Fury, you might think it's a sign or fate or whatever, but it's not. It's just a fucked-up situation."

Warner stares at me but says nothing.

"I just wanted to say that I've accepted a job from Jana to work for Florida Fury as their hype person, so we're going to have to interact with each other. I don't want it to be awkward, although I know it will be. I'm just asking if we can be decent with one another. I'll talk to Ford."

Although I'm fairly sure his friendship with Ford is dead. There's no way that's healing, ever.

"I was jealous last night too. Don't you see what that means?"

"It means nothing." I suck back the tears that want to spill. I never had a proper goodbye with Warner, so this almost feels like a weird closure.

He slides to the end of his seat. "It means everything, Gen. Do you think you'll ever feel for someone else the way you do me? Never. I tried for years to stay away, but not anymore. The minute I saw you again, it was all still there."

"What?" I ask, knowing I shouldn't.

"All that excitement and warmth, and god, I just wanted to hold you because..."

"Because what?"

"You're my home. I might have left, and I was a jackass beyond jackasses, but I left my heart with you and I'm never accepting it back. You know that. Deep down, you know, Imogen."

I stand, unable to continue this conversation. "I have to catch a flight back."

Warner rises from his chair and reaches out, but I pull back.

"Admit it," he pleads.

"There's nothing there. It died the minute you left."

The hope in his blue eyes shatters and is quickly replaced with sadness. "I know that's not true."

I pick up my purse. "It is. Let's just be civil and stop playing these games. Stop chasing me, because I don't want to be caught."

"Imogen," he says, and I stop a few steps away from him. "You know me. You know me better than anyone. So why would you think I'd walk away from something I want? I never have, and I don't plan on it now."

I turn around, keeping my tears at bay for just a little longer. "That's where you're wrong, Warner. You walked away from me when I was all yours. You walked away for a different life, and that's on you. So all I'm asking is for you to allow me to live in peace."

He stares at me, his jaw clenching because we both know I told the truth. "Never. I made the mistake once and I won't do it again. You know we're meant to be together, and I'm going to prove it to you."

"Then you'll fail every time."

I turn around and walk fast toward the lobby to catch my Uber. He doesn't chase me, but I feel his eyes on me until I disappear around the corner. And knowing he can't see me, I cling to the wall, closing my eyes and taking a deep breath.

Everything he said was right. I know I hold his heart, and he sure as hell still holds mine.

The End

ABOUT PIPER & RAYNE

Piper Rayne is a USA Today Bestselling Author duo who write "heartwarming humor with a side of sizzle" about families, whether that be blood or found. They both have e-readers full of one-clickable books, they're married to husbands who drive them to drink, and they're both chauffeurs to their kids. Most of all, they love hot heroes and quirky heroines who make them laugh, and they hope you do, too!

ALSO BY PIPER RAYNE

Hockey Hotties

Countdown to a Kiss (Free Novella)

My Lucky #13

The Trouble with #9

Faking it with #41

Sneaking around with #34

Second Shot with #76

Offside with #55

The Baileys

Lessons from a One-Night Stand

Advice from a Jilted Bride

Birth of a Baby Daddy

Operation Bailey Wedding (Novella)

Falling for My Brother's Best Friend

Demise of a Self-Centered Playboy

Confessions of a Naughty Nanny

Operation Bailey Babies (Novella)

Secrets of the World's Worst Matchmaker

Winning My Best Friend's Girl

Rules for Dating your Ex

Operation Bailey Birthday (Novella)

The Greenes

My Twist of Fortune (FREE)

My Beautiful Neighbor

My Almost Ex

My Vegas Groom

The Greene Family Summer Bash

My Sister's Flirty Friend

My Unexpected Surprise

My Famous Frenemy

The Greene Family Vacation

My Scorned Best Friend

My Fake Fiancé

My Brother's Forbidden Friend

The Modern Love World

Charmed by the Bartender

Hooked by the Boxer

Mad about the Banker

Complete Set (all 3 books)

The Single Dad's Club

Real Deal

Dirty Talker

Sexy Beast

Complete Set (all 3 books)

Hollywood Hearts

Mister Mom

Animal Attraction

Domestic Bliss

Bedroom Games

Cold as Ice

On Thin Ice

Break the Ice

Complete Set (all 3 books +)

Charity Case

Manic Monday

Afternoon Delight

Happy Hour

Complete Set (all 3 books)

Blue Collar Brothers

Flirting with Fire

Crushing on the Cop

Engaged to the EMT

Complete Set (All 3 books)

White Collar Brothers

Sexy Filthy Boss

Dirty Flirty Enemy

Wild Steamy Hook-up

The Rooftop Crew

My Bestie's Ex

A Royal Mistake

The Rival Roomies

Our Star-Crossed Kiss

The Do-Over

A Co-Workers Crush

Hockey Hotties

Countdown to a Kiss (Free Novella)

My Lucky #13

The Trouble with #9

Faking it with #41

Sneaking around with #34

Second Shot with #76

Offside with #55